MEGA MISSION!

By Ace Landers

ISBN 978-0-545-54121-3

12 11 10 9 8 7 6 5 4 3 2 1   13 14 15 16 17 18/0

Printed in the U.S.A.   40

First printing, July 2013

SCHOLASTIC INC.

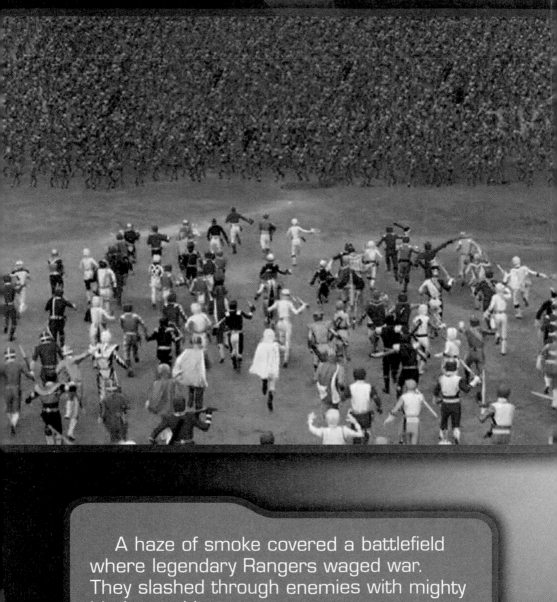

A haze of smoke covered a battlefield where legendary Rangers waged war. They slashed through enemies with mighty blades and lasers.

Then, as the mega clash furiously seethed, a metal warrior rose from the ashes of battle. The gleaming, menacing machine walked closer and closer until . . .

"Hey, New Kid," shouted the school-bus driver.

Troy suddenly woke up. He must have dozed off. "Whoa, that was a weird dream."

"You're gonna be late on the first day," the bus driver reminded him.

"Don't want that," said Troy, as he hopped off the bus and darted into school.

Inside, Mr. Burley was talking to his science class. "Okay, students, today's science brainteaser is: What species will outlast all others on Earth?"

Emma raised her hand and answered eagerly, "Insects! They'll survive all the bad stuff we're doing to the environment. They'll be the last ones standing."

"She's wrong, wrong, wrong," mumbled Noah from the back of the room.

"Calm down," said Jake, trying to shush his friend.

"Yes, Noah," said Mr. Burley. "You have a different answer?"

"ROBOTS!" blurted out Noah. "Robots powered by perpetual motion engines."

The students burst out laughing.

Gia, a beautiful and confident girl, chimed in. "Robots are machines. Technically, they're not a species."

"Wow, she's beautiful *and* smart," sighed Jake under the other student's laughter.

"And wrong," sulked Noah.

Just then, Troy entered the room, late for class.

"Troy, nice of you to join us," said Mr. Burley. "Maybe you can answer our brainteaser . . . what species will survive all others?"

Without hesitation, Troy answered, "Us. Humans. If humans work together, we can overcome anything."

Meanwhile, a mysterious spaceship secretly hovered in space.

Inside, evil insectoid aliens named Admiral Malkor, Vrak, and Creepox plotted to take over the Earth.

"From what I've seen so far during my time on Earth, they can't match our insect strength," cackled Creepox. "This planet will be a pushover."

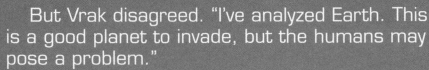

But Vrak disagreed. "I've analyzed Earth. This is a good planet to invade, but the humans may pose a problem."

"Humans are used to the smaller, harmless insects on their planet, but wait until we land!" boasted Admiral Malkor. "We will remove these humans from it and take this 'Earth' for ourselves!"

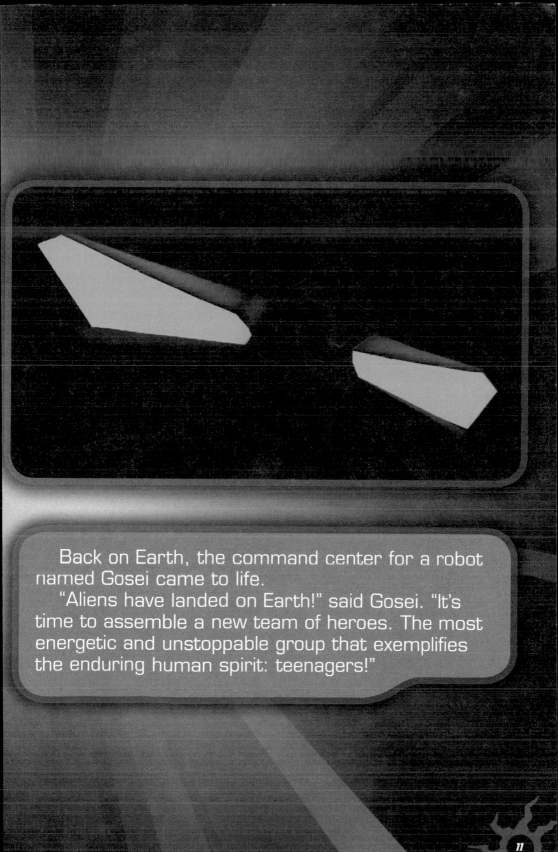

Back on Earth, the command center for a robot named Gosei came to life.

"Aliens have landed on Earth!" said Gosei. "It's time to assemble a new team of heroes. The most energetic and unstoppable group that exemplifies the enduring human spirit: teenagers!"

After school, Gia went to Ernie's Brain Freeze for a frozen-yogurt treat. What she didn't know was that the love-struck Jake and his best friend, Noah, had followed her there.

"She's the most popular girl in school," Noah explained. "Do you really think you have a chance with her, Jake?"

Meanwhile, Emma was in the forest taking pictures of butterflies. But instead of discovering butterflies, Emma spied a giant orange bug walking among the trees. "What is that?"

The bug stopped and sniffed the air. "I smell a human. . . ."

Without warning, Emma mysteriously vanished.

Back at Ernie's, Jake finally worked up the courage to talk to Gia, but she had disappeared.

As Jake scanned the room for Gia, Noah suddenly disappeared, too. "Noah? Where are you?"

And before Jake knew what was happening, he also vanished in a blast of light.

The loner Troy was busy that afternoon, too, practicing martial arts. His focus was intense as he snapped acrobatic kicks, rocked roundhouses, and threw well-trained punches at pretend enemies. Then, as he leaped into a giant flying kick, Troy also vanished — in a glowing light just like the others.

As quickly as the teens disappeared, they all reappeared together in a dark room.

"What just happened?!" exclaimed Jake.

"I'm not sure," said Noah, "but it was scientifically impossible and totally awesome!"

As the teens stood up, something appeared from the shadows. "Wow!" said Noah. "An old-school robot!"

The lights in the room illuminated as a booming voice announced, "Welcome, humans."
The room was a high-tech command center with a display that housed a row of action figures. At the front of the room was a giant tiki face.
"Freaky-tiki! I don't believe it!" said Jake.

The figure on the wall suddenly spoke. "I am Gosei, guardian of this planet since the beginning of time. Aliens have already landed, and *you* have been chosen to protect the Earth."

The teens all looked at one another in awe and confusion.

"He's not kidding!" said Emma, showing the photo of Creepox that she'd taken.

Gia studied the photo. "This can't be real!"

"This is all too real," answered Gosei. "You have been selected to form a team in the tradition of the Power Rangers. You shall protect the Earth as the Megaforce!"

"Emma," Gosei began, "you are a great gymnast. You shall be the Pink Ranger.

"Noah," continued Gosei, "your thirst for knowledge is unequaled. You shall be the Blue Ranger."

Then Gosei turned to Jake. "Your boundless athleticism and enthusiasm is unmatched, Jake. I am making you the Black Ranger.

"Gia," said Gosei, "you always pursue excellence. You will be the Yellow Ranger.

"And, Troy, you shall be the Red Ranger, the Dragon, and team leader."

Then Gosei gave each of the teens a small communicator that looked like Gosei. "These are your Mega Morphers. With them you will morph into Mega Rangers."

Troy looked at the others, and there was an unsaid agreement in the room. "Okay, if the Earth is under attack and you think we're the ones to protect it, then we're in."

Suddenly, Gosei's eyes started to glow. "Megaforce, your mission starts now. Believe in yourselves!"

The teens flashed to the edge of town only to come face-to-face with an army of alien soldiers called Loogies.

The soldiers surrounded the teens, but Troy attacked first, swiftly taking down two Loogies.

Everyone started fighting, but the soldiers were too powerful to defeat.

Troy yelled, "Gosei told us that the Morphers will give us power! Let's use them!"

"Go, go, Megaforce!" they shouted as they morphed into the Power Rangers Megaforce!

The Red Ranger led the attack. The foot soldiers burst into wet globs of green goo. But more Loogies appeared, no matter how many were defeated.

The Rangers were outnumbered, but that didn't stop them. First, the Black and Yellow Rangers set off a Mega Quake that cracked the road open and swallowed the alien foot soldiers whole.

Then the Blue Ranger used his Power Card to blast the soldiers with geysers of water.

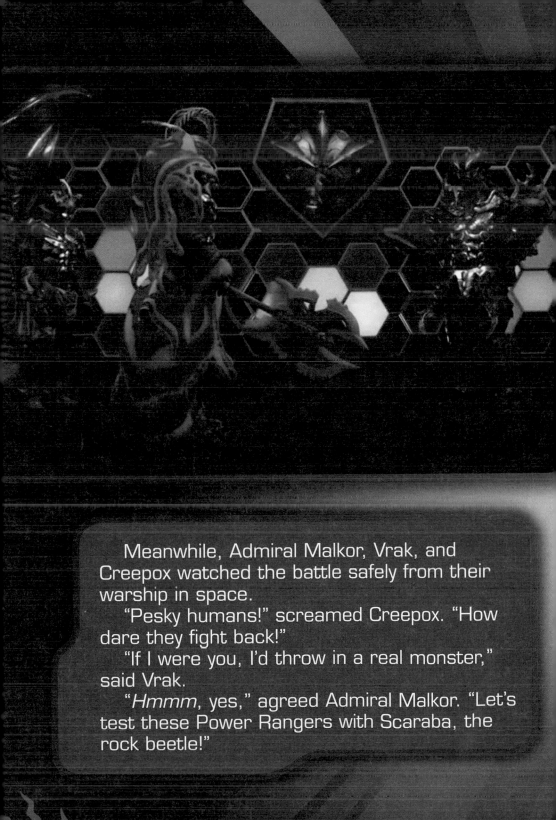

Meanwhile, Admiral Malkor, Vrak, and Creepox watched the battle safely from their warship in space.

"Pesky humans!" screamed Creepox. "How dare they fight back!"

"If I were you, I'd throw in a real monster," said Vrak.

"*Hmmm*, yes," agreed Admiral Malkor. "Let's test these Power Rangers with Scaraba, the rock beetle!"

Back on Earth, a giant beetle-like alien appeared showering the city with falling rubble.

"Hey, monster! If you wanna squash *them*, you'll have to get through *us*," yelled the Red Ranger. "We're the Power Rangers Megaforce!"

"Power Rangers?" the big bug scoffed. "Watch what happens when you get in a bug's way!" Then Scaraba blasted the Rangers with monstrous rubble boulders, but they dodged the attack.

Then, even more soldiers bubbled up from the ground.

The Power Rangers needed to use their Zords.

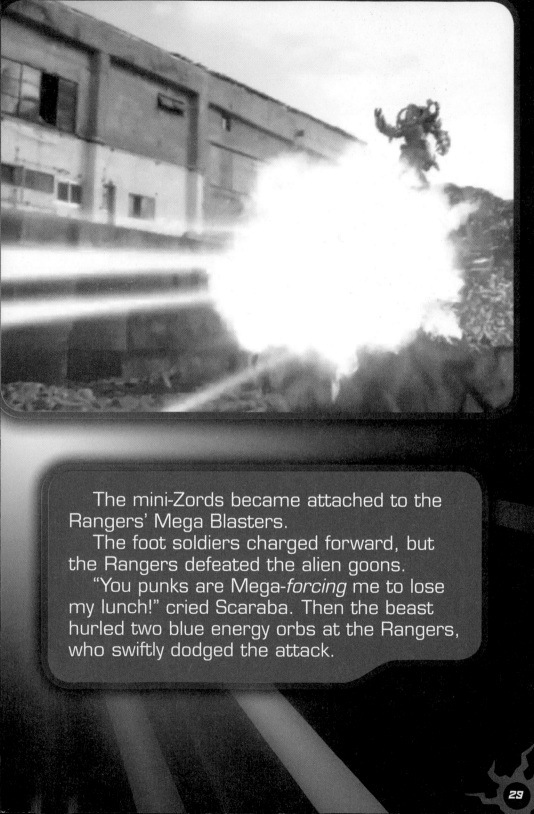

The mini-Zords became attached to the Rangers' Mega Blasters.

The foot soldiers charged forward, but the Rangers defeated the alien goons.

"You punks are Mega-*forcing* me to lose my lunch!" cried Scaraba. Then the beast hurled two blue energy orbs at the Rangers, who swiftly dodged the attack.

Now it was the Rangers' turn to fight back. First, the Red and Pink Rangers flew forward with a Dragon Sword and Phoenix Shot attack. Then the Black Ranger and the Yellow Ranger swiped Scaraba with a Snake Venom and Tiger Claw strike. Finally, the Blue Ranger smacked the alien bug with a Shark Bite beat down.

With Scaraba caught off guard, the Red Ranger announced, "Rangers, it's time to show true Mega Power."

All the Rangers' weapons assembled together in the Red Ranger's hand. It was the Megaforce Blaster! The Rangers each added their special Power Cards to power the weapon to full force.

Then the Rangers blasted Scaraba and wiped the alien off the face of the Earth.

"Megaforce, that's a mega win," declared the Red Ranger.

"Congratulations on a job well-done," said Gosei to the new team. "This morning you were regular kids leading normal lives. But now you must prepare to live extraordinary lives. You are the Power Rangers Megaforce."